Betsey Biggalow

the Detective

Also by Malorie Blackman

Betsey Biggalow

the Detective

Malorie
Blackman

Illustrated by Jamie Smith

RED FOX

BETSEY BIGGALOW THE DETECTIVE
A RED FOX BOOK 978 1 782 95184 1

First published in Great Britain in 1992 by Piccadilly Press Ltd

This edition published by Red Fox, an imprint of
Random House Children's Publishers UK
A Random House Group Company

This Red Fox edition published 2014

1 3 5 7 9 10 8 6 4 2

Text copyright © Oneta Malorie Blackman, 1992
Illustrations copyright © Jamie Smith, 2014

The Random House Group Limited supports the Forest Stewardship Council® (FSC®),
the leading international forest-certification organisation. Our books carrying the FSC
label are printed on FSC®-certified paper. FSC is the only forest-certification scheme
supported by the leading environmental organisations, including Greenpeace. Our paper
procurement policy can be found at www.randomhouse.co.uk/environment.

MIX
Paper from
responsible sources
FSC® C016897

Set in Bembo MT

RANDOM HOUSE CHILDREN'S PUBLISHERS UK
61–63 Uxbridge Road, London W5 5SA

www.randomhousechildrens.co.uk
www.totallyrandombooks.co.uk
www.randomhouse.co.uk

Addresses for companies within The Random House Group Limited can be found at:
www.randomhouse.co.uk/offices.htm

THE RANDOM HOUSE GROUP Limited Reg. No. 954009

A CIP catalogue record for this book is available from the British Library.

Printed and bound in Great Britain by CPI Group (UK) Ltd, Croydon CR0 4YY

For Neil and Lizzy,
with love as always.

Malorie Blackman has written over sixty books and is acknowledged as one of today's most imaginative and convincing writers for young readers. She has been awarded numerous prizes for her work, including the Red House Children's Book Award and the Fantastic Fiction Award. Malorie has also been shortlisted for the Carnegie Medal. In 2005 she was honoured with the Eleanor Farjeon Award in recognition of her contribution to children's books, and in 2008 she received an OBE for her services to children's literature. She has been described by *The Times* as 'a national treasure'. Malorie Blackman is the Children's Laureate 2013–15.

Contents

Betsey and the Soft Landing

"Sherena, can I ride your bicycle? Please, *please*?"

"No, Betsey," Sherena replied. "It's too big for you. You'd never get your feet on the pedals anyway."

"I would if you helped me," Betsey said.

"No," said Sherena firmly. "You're only used to four-wheel bikes."

"No, I'm not. I've ridden on May's bike and that's only got two wheels. Please, Sherena."

1

"My bike is a lot bigger than May's," said Sherena.

"But I want to get some exercise," Betsey tried.

"Go for a walk then," said Sherena.

"But Sherena . . ." Betsey began.

"Betsey, I said no and I mean no," said Sherena. "I didn't save up all my money for over two years and work every week-end and completely remake a second-hand bike just so you could wreck it for me."

"Botheration, Sherena! You're so mean," said Betsey, crossly.

"And you're such a pest," replied Sherena. And off she walked.

Betsey went out into the front yard. There was Sherena's bike, lying on its side, and Betsey wanted to ride on it. She wanted to ride on it something fierce! Oh, to ride with the wind on her face and the pedals racing round, going fast, fast, *fast*. Betsey walked over to the bike. She lifted it up, holding on to the handlebars. Maybe if she just sat on it . . . Just for a minute. Just for a moment.

"Oh, if only I had a bike of my own . . ." Betsey whispered. Then she could ride and ride – all the way across Barbados and back!

Betsey leaned the bike towards her, her hands on the handlebars. She squeezed the brakes. The bike felt *wonderful*.

"I'll just have a quick sit on it," Betsey decided. After all, one teeny, tiny sit wouldn't hurt. Betsey began to swing her right leg over the bike.

"Betsey Biggalow! I hope you're not thinking of riding that thing." Gran'ma Liz appeared from nowhere to stand on the front porch.

"No, Gran'ma Liz," said Betsey quickly. "Of course not."

Betsey hopped off the bike.

"I should think not," said Gran'ma. "If the good Lord had meant for us to go tearing around on a bicycle, then we would have wheels instead of legs."

Gran'ma Liz didn't approve of bikes.

"Come on in, child," said Gran'ma. "You haven't finished all your chores yet."

So Betsey went inside the house. But for the rest of the day, everything Betsey saw reminded her of Sherena's bike. Round things like plug holes and the tops of tins all reminded her of the wheels on her sister's bike. When Betsey went into her bedroom, the door handle reminded her of the bike's handlebars. When Betsey sat down, she wondered if the saddle of Sherena's bike was as firm, as comfortable.

Finally Betsey could stand it no more.

"Botheration!" Betsey muttered to herself. "I want to ride that bike and I'm *going* to ride that bike."

After dinner, Betsey went out into the front yard. The bike was still there, lying on the ground. Betsey picked it up and stroked it.

"If you were my bike, I'd look after you better than this," Betsey whispered.

"Hi, Betsey. What are you doing? Talking to your sister's bike?" Betsey's good friend May appeared, making Betsey jump.

"May . . ." Betsey put her finger over her lips. "Don't tell anyone but I'm off for a ride."

"You can't." May stared. "Sherena's bike is much too big for you. You'll fall off and break every bone in your body!"

"No, I won't. I'm good at this," Betsey argued.

"How many times have you ridden on it?" May asked.

"Er . . . this will be the first time," Betsey admitted. "But it can't be much more difficult than riding your bike. You just sit down on the saddle and hold on to the handlebars and pedal."

"Betsey . . ." May began.

"Botheration, May, are you going to help me or not?" asked Betsey.

"Oh, all right then," May said at last. "But be careful."

"You can be my lookout. Tell me if

anyone's coming." Betsey swung her leg over the bike. She grinned at May.

"Here I go!" Betsey laughed and she jumped up to sit on the saddle, her feet on the pedals.

The bike wibbled and wobbled while Betsey tried to steady it.

"I'm doing it! I'm riding!" Betsey squealed with delight. "And Sherena said my feet wouldn't reach the pedals! My sister doesn't know what she's talking about!"

"Shhh!" May warned, looking around.

"I'm going to ride down the footpath to the beach and back," said Betsey. And

off she went, pedalling furiously.

"Betsey, no! COME BACK!" May called after her.

Betsey hardly heard her friend. The warm wind was on her face and the pedals were racing round and round. It was even more fun than Betsey had thought it would be.

"What's all the shouting about?" Sherena came out of the house. Then she saw Betsey – and her bike – disappearing into the distance. "My bike! Betsey! I told you that you couldn't ride it. Just wait till I catch you," Sherena yelled.

Betsey turned her head to look at her big sister. That was a big, BIG mistake! The bike started to wobble and to wibble even more than before. Betsey squeezed the brakes. The bike started to slow down, but then Betsey realised something. Her legs *were* long enough to reach the pedals, but they *weren't* long enough to reach the ground. Sitting on the saddle meant that she could only reach the pedals. How was she going to stop the bike without falling

on the hard ground and hurting herself?

"Sherena! May! HELP!" Betsey shouted.

"Hang on, Betsey!" Sherena raced after her sister.

"We're coming!" May dashed after Sherena.

Betsey stuck her legs out straight in front of her, but she didn't dare squeeze the brakes very hard. Now Betsey was on the beach. Sand flew up everywhere. And she was heading for the sea.

"I don't want to get wet!" Betsey shrieked. She decided she'd rather fall on the sand than in the sea, so she pressed the brakes – hard!

Too hard. Betsey went flying over the handlebars and both she and the bike fell – SPLOOSH! – into the water. The bike lay on its side, the back wheel spinning around. Betsey sat in the water, shaking her head and wondering what had happened.

She was sitting in only a few centimetres of water but it was wet and felt yukky! Sherena and May came running up.

"Betsey, are you all right?" Sherena asked anxiously.

Betsey stood up, her shirt and trousers soaked. "I . . . I think so," she said.

"Well, you won't be when I've finished with you," Sherena said angrily. "I told you not to ride on my bike."

"Don't worry, Sherena." Betsey shook her head. "I'm not even going to sit on it again until my legs grow at least another ten centimetres!"

Sherena made Betsey pick up the bike and *push* it all the way back to the house.

"And when we get home, you can dry it and clean it and oil it too," said Sherena.

And for once Betsey didn't argue.

"Never mind, Betsey," whispered May. "You didn't break every bone in your body like I thought you would!"

"The sea gave me a nice, soft landing," Betsey whispered back. "It's just a shame my landing was so *wet* as well!"

The Best Show
in the World

Betsey stretched her hands out in front of her, before resting them on the keyboard.

"I'm now going to make up a song off the top of my head and play it for you," said Betsey very importantly. Then she plonked her hands up and down the keyboard, running them over the black and white keys.

"Betsey, no more — please," Sherena begged. "You are driving me up the wall, round the twist and off my head! That noise you're making is *horrible*!"

"It's not noise. It's music!" said Betsey

and she started playing again.

"My name is Betsey,
And I live in a house.
I don't have a cat,
And I don't have a mouse!
Yeah! Yeah! Yeah!"

It sounded good to her!

Prince, the family black and brown Alsatian dog, raised his head and began to howl.

"Hoooo! Owww-owww!" yowled Prince.

"Betsey, I'll give you anything you want if you'll just hush up!" pleaded Desmond. "Look, you're even getting on Prince's nerves now!"

"Botheration, Desmond! You don't know good music when you hear it." Betsey frowned. "And I'm not getting on Prince's nerves. He's singing along with me."

PLONK! PLINK! PLONK! Betsey banged on the keyboard even louder than before. Playing the keyboard was such fun! The music sounded really good – and the louder she played, the better it sounded! Dad bought the keyboard for all of them, before he'd had to leave to finish his final year of studying. Dad was going to be a doctor.

Just then the front door opened and in walked Mum and Gran'ma Liz.

"Mum, make her stop! Please make her stop!" wailed Sherena.

"She's driving us bonkers!" Desmond moaned, his hands over his ears.

"Look, Mum! Listen, Gran'ma Liz! I've made up a song," said Betsey. She ran her fingers up and down the keyboard.

"My name is Betsey,
And I live in a house.
I don't have a cat,
And I don't have a mouse!
Yeah! Yeah! Yeah!"

"Isn't that brilliant?" Betsey asked.

"It's very good, Betsey." Mum started to shake her head, then quickly turned it into a nod.

"Lovely, child," said Gran'ma Liz, weakly. "But don't you think the keyboard should have a rest now?"

"Oh no, Gran'ma. This keyboard is the best present in the world and it's going to last for ever and ever," said Betsey. "Besides, I need to practise."

"Why?" asked Mum.

"May and I are going to put on a show for all of you," announced Betsey. "It's going to be the best show in the whole world!"

"Oh-oh!" Sherena muttered.

"I don't like the sound of that," Desmond mumbled.

"Betsey, I think you should have asked us first," said Mum.

"Why?" asked Betsey.

"Because . . . because . . ." But Mum couldn't think of a single reason!

For the next few days, May came over in the afternoons after school. May and Betsey sat in front of the keyboard giggling and playing *music* – at least that's what they both called it!

The next day was Saturday. Mum invited some of her friends and neighbours over and soon there were grown-ups in almost every part of the living room. But

to Mum and Gran'ma Liz's surprise, other people started arriving at the house as well. First there was May, then came Josh and Celeste and others from Betsey's class.

"You're all welcome but what's going on?" asked Mum.

"We've come to see Betsey's show," Josh replied.

"Betsey's show!" Mum's eyes opened wide like saucers. Mum turned to look at Betsey. "Elizabeth Ruby Biggalow, I want a word with you in your room."

Ooops! Whenever Mum used Betsey's whole, full name then Betsey knew that she was in for some *serious* talking!

"Why didn't you tell me that you'd invited all your friends over to hear your show?" Mum asked. "And why didn't you tell me that you were putting on your show *today*?"

"Sorry, Mum," said Betsey. "I thought it would be fun to put on a show for the grown-ups as well, as a sort of surprise."

"Did you? Well, you should have told me first," said Mum.

"Your friends will like it, Mum." Betsey smiled. "It's going to be the best show in the world."

"Hhmm!" was all Mum said.

Betsey walked back to the keyboard. "Are you ready?" she whispered to May.

May swallowed hard, then nodded. "I think so."

Betsey stood up. "Ladies and gentle-men," she began grandly. "Please take your seats. May and I are going to put on a show for you. We've been practising and practising."

"I'm off! I'm going to my friend Marlon's house," said Desmond.

"You can't go now," said Betsey. "Please, we're just about to start. Mum, tell him!"

"Desmond, wait until your sister's show is over," said Mum.

"Do I have to?" groaned Desmond.

"Give her a chance," Mum replied.

"Desmond, you'll like it. Honest!" said Betsey.

Desmond muttered something under his breath. It sounded like, "Bet I don't!" but it could have been, "No, I won't!"

May and Betsey sat next to each other and placed their hands on the keys. Betsey slid the volume control up to maximum.

"This song is called *The Sing-Along Song!* Ready, everyone?" Betsey asked.

They all nodded. Betsey and May plonked their hands down on the keyboard and began to run their fingers

up and down the keys. Then they both started to sing:

"We're May and Betsey
We made up this song.
And with this song,
We can't go wrong!
This song is big
This song is strong.
This song is called a Sing-Along song!"

"This song is very, very long," whispered Sherena.

"Shush!" hissed Mum.

Betsey and May carried on singing.

"So if you really like this song,
Take a breath and sing along."

Betsey and May started singing their song from the beginning again and playing the keyboard at the same time. All their friends started singing first, while the grown-ups just looked at each other. Then something very strange happened.

Mum started it. She started singing along too! Then Gran'ma Liz joined in, saying, "If you can't beat 'em, join 'em." Sherena and Desmond looked around the room in amazement. All the other grownups were singing as well, huge, great grins on their faces.

"Oh well!" said Sherena. And with a laugh, both Desmond and Sherena started singing too. Desmond and Sherena gave out biscuits and cake and everyone had a lot of fun!

Later that day, Gran'ma Liz said, "Well done, Betsey. I *did* enjoy your show. I haven't laughed so much in a long, long time."

"I told you you'd enjoy it," said Betsey. "I told you it would be the best show in the world. And what's more, we're going to put on lots and lots more shows . . . We're going to put on a show every week from now on . . ."

"Mum!" Desmond and Sherena squealed.

"Quite right!" Mum smiled. "In fact, Betsey, I've been talking with Gran'ma Liz and we both think that as you're so keen, we'll find the money to send you for piano lessons with Mrs Paul from the other side of town. You can have one lesson every two weeks and practise every day. When you've learnt a few more songs, then you can put on another show."

"Lessons?" Betsey's jaw dropped. "Did you say lessons?"

"I certainly did," said Mum.

"Oh . . . lessons?" Betsey didn't sound too keen.

"Don't you want to learn how to play the keyboard properly?" asked Mum.

"I guess so. But lessons . . . Er, Mum, can I have a think about it?" asked Betsey.

"Of course you can. Take all the time you need." Mum smiled.

Funny, but that was the last time Betsey even touched the keyboard for a long, long while!

Betsey Biggalow, the Detective!

Betsey put down her book. So that's how Sam, the girl detective, found the missing money!

That was a good story, thought Betsey.

"Slinky, that was a great story." Betsey picked up the book to show to her teddy bear.

But Slinky wasn't there ... Botheration! Where was Slinky Malinky?

Betsey searched here and there and everywhere, but she just couldn't find her.

29

Slinky Malinky was a small, orange teddy bear with a lop-sided smile and round button eyes. Betsey didn't play with her teddy any more, but Slinky Malinky sat at the bottom of her bed and sometimes Betsey would talk to her. She'd had Slinky Malinky for a long, long time – ever since she could remember. Only now Slinky was missing. Where was she?

"There's only one thing for it," Betsey muttered to herself. "I'm going to have to become a detective, just like in my book, until I find her!"

Betsey had a long, hard think. Then she went into her bedroom and dug out a Sherlock Holmes hat from her dressing-up box. The hat had been part of a costume Sherena had worn for a fancy dress party. It was far too big for Betsey, so she had to tilt it well back off her forehead. Next she got one of Sherena's old notepads and a pencil.

But there was still something missing. Betsey wandered into Gran'ma Liz's room. And there she saw it – Gran'ma Liz's magnifying glass! Gran'ma Liz used the magnifying glass for inspecting lots of different flowers. Gran'ma Liz loved to study flowers. Betsey held it up to her face and tried to look through it but she couldn't see a thing – everything was all blurred. She prac-
tised moving the glass between her face and the flowers Gran'ma had pressed in one of her flower books until they appeared big and clear. She could see all kinds of details using the magnifying glass that she hadn't

seen before. Now she knew how to use it. Betsey looked at herself in the mirror. Perfect! She was all set. Now she looked just like a detective! She looked just like a real detective in one of those programmes Gran'ma Liz liked watching on TV so much. Betsey ran back into her bedroom.

Clues. The first thing to do was to search for clues. Here was one! Betsey found Slinky's red ribbon under the window. It should have been tied in a bow around her teddy's neck . . .

"What next?" Betsey wondered. And off she went into the living room.

"Good grief, Betsey. What are you supposed to be?" asked Gran'ma Liz, looking up from her book.

"I'm a detective just like on TV," said Betsey.

"Is that my magnifying glass?" Gran'ma Liz frowned.

Betsey nodded. "I'll be very careful with it, Gran'ma Liz – honest," she said quickly.

"Hhmm! Well, just make sure you are," said Gran'ma Liz. "So what can I do for you, Detective Biggalow?"

"I'd like to ask you a few questions," said Betsey.

"Go on then." Gran'ma Liz smiled.

"Gran'ma, when was the last time you saw Slinky Malinky?" asked Betsey.

"Hhmm! Well now . . . let me see . . ." Gran'ma Liz lowered her book and pondered.

"It was . . . it must have been three nights ago when your Mum was working late. I tucked you in and read you a story – remember? Wasn't Slinky Malinky at the bottom of your bed then?"

Betsey wrote down "GRAN'MA LIZ" in her book and underlined it three times. Under that she wrote, "Three nights ago on my bed."

"Thanks, Gran'ma Liz," said Betsey, her hat slipping down to cover her eyes.

"Sherena's head is the size of a planet!" said Betsey. "This Sherlock Holmes hat is massive!"

"The hat you're wearing is called a deerstalker," Gran'ma Liz said.

"Deerstalker! How funny!" Betsey laughed and off she went to find her bigger brother. Desmond was in the back yard, bowling a cricket ball to his friend Sam. Betsey went and stood right in between them.

"Desmond, when was the last time you saw Slinky Malinky?" Betsey asked.

"Your teddy bear?" Desmond frowned.

"That's right," replied Betsey.

"I haven't a clue when I last saw Slinky," Desmond said.

Betsey wrote down "DESMOND" in her notebook and underlined it three times.

"Desmond, how do you spell 'unhelpful'?" Betsey asked. Desmond told her. Betsey wrote "UNHELPFUL" in great big capital letters under his name.

"Why have you got on that funny hat?" Desmond asked.

"It's called a deerstalker and I'm wearing it because I'm Betsey Biggalow, the Great Detective, and detectives always wear hats," answered Betsey.

"Your sister is a nut!" Sam said to Desmond.

Desmond shook his head. "I know. I hope it's not catching!"

Betsey ignored them and rushed off. She didn't feel any closer to finding Slinky Malinky. Betsey ran to see her bigger sister. Sherena was doing her homework.

"Sherena, when was the last time you saw Slinky Malinky?" Betsey asked.

"Who are you supposed to be?" Sherena laughed.

"I'm a detective. And I should be asking the questions, not you," said Betsey.

Sherena raised her eyebrows. "Excuse me!"

"Well, when was the last time you saw Slinky Malinky?" Betsey repeated.

"Yesterday," Sherena remembered. "She was on my bed, so I threw her back onto yours."

"Hhmm!" Betsey wrote "SHERENA" in her notepad and underlined it three times. Under that she wrote, "Yesterday on her bed." But that gave Betsey an idea.

Betsey went back to her bedroom. She took off her hat and walked over to Sherena's bed. Where would Slinky have landed when Sherena threw her across the room? Betsey folded up her Sherlock hat until it was Slinky-sized. Then she squatted on Sherena's bed until she was Sherena's height and threw the hat across the room. The hat bounced off Betsey's bed to land behind it. Betsey raced across the room. This had to be it! Slinky must be behind the bed.

Betsey pulled her bed further away from the wall . . . and how strange! Slinky wasn't there, but some of Slinky's stuffing was. Betsey recognised it at once. And next to the stuffing were some longish, dark brown hairs . . . The hairs looked strangely familiar . . . Betsey put the Sherlock hat back on and picked up her two new clues. She put Slinky's stuffing in her pocket, but she held on to the hairs.

"I bet these belong to the person who kidnapped Slinky," said Betsey.

She went into the living room and, using the magnifying glass, checked them against Gran'ma Liz's hair. Gran'ma Liz's hair was longish, but grey, not brown. Betsey held up her newest clue to Sherena's head, but Sherena's hair was jet black and long. Betsey compared the hairs she'd found to Desmond's hair but Desmond's hair was shorter and curlier.

Betsey even tried matching the hairs she'd found against Sam's head, but they didn't match either. Sam had even less hair than Desmond!

Betsey put down the magnifying glass and sat down on a kitchen chair with her head in her hands. Botheration! Now what should she do? She'd asked Gran'ma Liz and Desmond and Sherena about Slinky Malinky and none of them knew where her teddy was. Mum was at work so there was no one else to ask – unless you included Prince, the Alsatian dog. Prince was there, lying under the window.

"It's a pity you can't talk to me, Prince," sighed Betsey. "Maybe then you could tell me when you last saw my teddy bear."

"Woooof!" barked Prince, and out he ran into the back yard.

Betsey looked down at the hairs in her

hand, then out of the kitchen window at Prince, then back down at the hairs.

"Got it! I know who did it!" exclaimed Betsey. She dashed out into the yard. Sam and Desmond were still playing cricket. Prince was at the back of the yard digging furiously.

"Desmond! Sam! Quick! It's Prince. Prince kidnapped Slinky Malinky!" Betsey shouted, chasing down the yard after Prince.

"How do you know that?" Desmond frowned.

"I found some of Prince's hairs in my bedroom, along with some of Slinky's stuffing. I'm sure it's Prince," said Betsey. "Prince, you bad dog, what have you done with my teddy bear?"

"Woooo-oooooof!" barked Prince, digging even more furiously than before.

At that very second, Prince raised his head, his tail wagging faster than fast. And what did he have in his mouth? Slinky Malinky! A very dirty, dusty Slinky Malinky who was a lot skinnier than the last time Betsey saw her!

"Prince, you ought to be ashamed," said Betsey. "You're the kidnapper! I knew these dark brown hairs belonged to you! I'm not going to pat you for finding my teddy when you buried her in the first place!"

Betsey took her teddy away from Prince. Slinky Malinky was filthy.

"I'll have to get Mum to wash her now." Betsey frowned.

"And look what else is in here." Desmond pointed to the hole that Prince had just dug. "That's Mum's tape measure . . . and Gran'ma Liz's perfume bottle . . ."

"Desmond, isn't that your school book?" asked Sam.

"Yes it is!" said Desmond, surprised. "My teacher told me off because I couldn't find it. Prince, you bad dog!"

"I told you I was a great detective," said Betsey. "Not only did I rescue Slinky Malinky, but I found things I didn't even know I was looking for in the first place!"

Betsey Flies a Kite

Gran'ma Liz was busy hanging out the clothes on the washing line. Desmond and Betsey were sitting at the bottom of the garden, their heads bent over something.

"Desmond, Betsey, I thought you two were going to help me with the washing," said Gran'ma Liz.

"Sorry, Gran'ma Liz. We forgot," said Betsey. "We will next time – we promise."

"What are you up to then? You've both been really quiet all morning," said Gran'ma Liz. "That's why I didn't call you. It was worth not having your help for the peace and quiet I got instead!"

"I'm showing Betsey how to make something," said Desmond. "Because I'm the best brother in the whole world!"

"And the most modest! Well, whatever you do, mind the clothes. I've only just washed them and they're not dry yet," Gran'ma Liz said.

"We won't go anywhere near the clothes, Gran'ma – honest!" said Betsey.

"Hhmm! Just make sure you don't," sniffed Gran'ma Liz. And she walked back into the house.

"Right then. Let's make sure we've got everything we need," said Desmond. "Have we got string?"

"We've got a huge ball of string. Here it is," replied Betsey.

"Just say 'check', Betsey or we'll be here

all day." Desmond smiled. "Now then, we need two long, straight branches, one slightly longer than the other."

"Got them. Check!" said Betsey.

"Strong, coloured tissue paper?"

"Check!"

"Sticky tape?"

"Check!"

"Some old pieces of ribbon?" Desmond asked.

"I got these from Mum. Check!" answered Betsey.

"Scissors?"

"Check!"

"Then we're all set," said Desmond.

"Hooray!" shouted Betsey. "We're going to make a kite!"

Desmond grinned. "The first thing to do is to make a cross using the branches. Then tie them together using some of the string."

"Check!" said Betsey. And she picked up the branches and laid the shorter one over the longer one. Then she got some string and tied the two branches together so that they formed a cross shape.

"Make sure you tie the string good and tight," said Desmond.

Betsey tied it very slowly and carefully, wrapping it round the branches, first one way, then the other. Then she tied the two ends of string in a tight knot.

"That's good," Desmond said. "Now we have to spread out the tissue paper and place the branches on it."

"Like this?" Betsey asked.

"That's right," replied Desmond.

For the next hour Desmond and Betsey worked at making a kite. They cut two large diamond shapes out of the flaming-red tissue paper and stuck them to the branches. They tied tiny bits of ribbon to a piece of string as long as Betsey's arm and then tied that on to the bottom of the kite. Then they attached one end of the ball of string to the bottom of the kite as well.

At last Desmond and Betsey jumped up. They had finished! They were ready to try it out. Betsey hopped up and down. She'd done it! She'd made her very first kite!

"Wooof!" Prince, the Alsatian dog, tried to sniff around the kite as Betsey held it up.

"No, Prince. Bad dog! That kite isn't for you," said Desmond.

"Where are we going to fly it?" Betsey asked excitedly.

"We can practise a few things here," Desmond decided. "Then we'll go to the beach and fly it really high."

"Will it swoop and soar and glide?" asked Betsey, her eyes wide.

"Of course it will." Desmond laughed. "We built it!"

"So what should we practise first?" Betsey asked.

"The run up," said Desmond. "Betsey, you stand here and hold the kite in your hands. Then run to the other end of the yard, letting the kite go at the same time. You've also got to let the string out as you run so that the kite has a chance to rise into the air. Have you got all that?"

It was a lot to remember all at once, but Betsey knew she could do it.

This is going to be easy, Betsey thought.

The only trouble was, as soon as she started running, Prince started chasing behind her.

"Wooof! Woooof!" barked Prince. He wanted to be part of the game too.

"Botheration, Prince! I'll never get this right if you don't behave yourself," said Betsey, crossly.

Betsey ran to the back of the yard to try again.

"Wooooof!" Prince chased behind her,

trying to leap up at the kite.

"Desmond!" Betsey pleaded.

Desmond held Prince's collar while Betsey did her run. The kite barely lifted higher than her waist before it collapsed to the ground.

"Run faster, Betsey," Desmond suggested. "And hold the kite up higher before you let it go."

"Check!" said Betsey, walking back to one end of the yard.

"Ready? GO!" shouted Desmond.

And off Betsey ran. She released the kite so that she was only holding on to it by its string and ran even faster. The kite flipped and flapped and fluttered, but it began to *rise*.

"Yippee! It's working! It's working," shouted Betsey.

"Yeah! Go Betsey! Go!" Desmond jumped up and down.

But oh dear! The kite got caught up in the washing line. Desmond was so busy jumping up and down that he forgot to hold onto Prince's collar. Prince raced across the yard and started jumping up at the kite, barking madly.

"No, Prince. DON'T . . ." squeaked Betsey.

She grabbed for Prince. Prince grabbed for the kite and . . . the whole washing line came tumbling down.

Oh no! Desmond and Betsey and Prince stared at the shirts and socks and underwear and dresses and trousers all over the ground.

"We're in trouble now . . ." Desmond sighed.

Sure enough, about two seconds later, Gran'ma Liz came storming out of the house.

"Desmond, Betsey, I thought I told you two to mind the washing," fumed Gran'ma Liz.

"But Gran'ma Liz, Prince . . ." Betsey began.

"It was Prince who . . ." Desmond tried.

"Not another word." Gran'ma Liz interrupted them both. "You two are going to help me wash every single one of these things again."

"Oh, but we wanted to fly our kite," said Betsey.

"Not a chance! Not until all the washing has been redone. And you can start by gathering it all up again," said Gran'ma Liz, and she marched back into the house.

Betsey and Desmond turned to Prince. Prince watched them, his tail between his legs, his head hanging down.

"Botheration, Prince!" said Betsey, crossly. "Double and triple botheration!"

"Woof!" Prince apologised.

"Well, you did promise Gran'ma that

we'd help her the next time she did the washing," Desmond reminded his sister.

"Yes," replied Betsey, "but I didn't think we'd be helping Gran'ma quite so soon!"

"Never mind," said Desmond. "Once we've loaded up the washing machine we'll go to the beach and try again."

"Promise?" said Betsey.

"Promise." Desmond smiled.

"And can we leave Prince at home this time?" said Betsey.

"Arfff! Arfff!" barked Prince. He didn't sound too keen on that idea.

"No, Prince, you're not coming with us," said Desmond firmly. "Not this time."

Betsey grinned at her brother. "Thanks for helping me make and fly a kite."

"Anything for my annoying little sister!" teased Desmond.

Betsey stood in front of Desmond and piled all the clothes in her arms on top of the ones Desmond was already carrying.

"Hey!" said Desmond. "What's the big idea?"

"I just wanted to give you something," said Betsey.

Before Desmond could say another word, Betsey gave him a great, big hug. She really did have the best brother in the world!